D0468204

`TWAS THE NIGHT BEFORE CHRISTMAS
and Other Holiday Favorites

Illustrated by
Greg Hildebrandt

The Unicorn Publishing House
New Jersey

For over a decade, Unicorn has been publishing richly
illustrated editions of classic and contemporary works
for children and adults. To continue this tradition,
WE WOULD LIKE TO KNOW WHAT YOU THINK.

If you would like to send us your suggestions or obtain
a list of our current titles, please write to:
THE UNICORN PUBLISHING HOUSE, INC.
P.O. BOX 377
Morris Plains, NJ 07950
ATT: Dept CLP

❖❖❖❖❖❖❖

© 1990 The Unicorn Publishing House. All Rights Reserved
Artwork © 1984 Greg Hildebrandt. All Rights Reserved
This book may not be reproduced in whole or in part, by any means,
without written permission. For information, contact: Jean L. Scrocco,
Unicorn Publishing House, 120 American Road, Morris Plains, NJ 07950
Printed in U.S.A.

Printing History 15 14 13 12 11 10 9 8 7 6 5 4 3 2

Library of Congress Cataloging–in–Publication Data

'Twas The Night Before Christmas and Other Holiday Favorites/ illustrated by Greg
  Hildebrandt.
  p.cm.—(Through the Magic Window series)
  Summary: Presents the familiar "Night Before Christmas," the story of the Nativity,
  and eight traditional Christmas carols with music.

  1. Christmas—Literary collections. [1. Christmas—Literary collections.]
  I. Hildebrandt, Greg, ill.   II. Series: Through the Magic Window.
  PZ5.T85 1990
  808.8'033—dc20
                                                                90-10976
                                                                    CIP
                                                                     AC

**T**was
the night
before
Christmas

CONCORDIA UNIVERSITY LIBRARY
PORTLAND, OR 97211

'Twas the night before Christmas,
When all through the house,
Not a creature was stirring, not even a mouse.

The stockings were hung by the chimney with care,
In hopes that St. Nicholas soon would be there.

The children were nestled all snug in their beds,
While visions of sugarplums danced in their heads.

And Mamma in her kerchief, and I in my cap,
Had just settled down for a long winter's nap.
When out on the lawn there arose such a clatter,
I sprang from my bed to see what was the matter.

Away to the window I flew like a flash,
Tore open the shutters and threw up the sash.

The moon on the breast of the new-fallen snow,
Gave a luster of midday to objects below,

When, what to my wondering eyes should appear,
But a miniature sleigh, and eight tiny reindeer,
With a little old driver, so lively and quick,
I knew in a moment it must be St. Nick.

More rapid than eagles his coursers they came,
And he whistled, and shouted, and called them by name:

"Now, Dasher! Now, Dancer! Now, Prancer and Vixen!
On, Comet! On, Cupid! On, Donder and Blitzen!
To the top of the porch! To the top of the wall!
Now, dash away! Dash away! Dash away all!"

As dry leaves that before the wild hurricane fly,
When they meet with an obstacle, mount to the sky,
So up to the housetop the coursers they flew,
With the sleigh full of toys, and St. Nicholas, too.

And then in a twinkling, I heard on the roof
The prancing and pawing of each little hoof.

As I drew in my head, and was turning around,
Down the chimney St. Nicholas came with a bound.

He was dressed all in fur, from his head to his foot,
And his clothes were all tarnished with ashes and soot.
A bundle of toys he had flung on his back,
And he looked like a peddler just opening his pack.

His eyes how they twinkled! His dimples how merry!
His cheeks were like roses, his nose like a cherry.
His droll little mouth was drawn up like a bow,
And the beard on his chin was as white as the snow.

The stump of a pipe he held tight in his teeth,
And the smoke, it encircled his head like a wreath.
He had a broad face and a little round belly.
That shook, when he laughed, like a bowl full of jelly.

He was chubby and plump, a right jolly old elf,
And I laughed when I saw him, in spite of myself.
A wink of his eye and a twist of his head,
Soon gave me to know I had nothing to dread.

He spoke not a word, but went straight to his work,
And filled all the stockings, then turned with a jerk,
And laying his finger aside of his nose,
And giving a nod, up the chimney he rose.

He sprang to his sleigh, to his team gave a whistle,
And away they all flew like the down of a thistle.

But I heard him exclaim as he drove out of sight,
"Happy Christmas to all, and to all a good night."

The
Nativity

In those days the kingdom of Judea was under the rule of the Romans. Although the Jewish people had their own laws, they also had to obey the laws of the Romans. The emperor of Rome, Caesar Augustus, decided he wanted a new tax on the people. So he ordered his soldiers to count all the people in the land. Each person was to go to the place of their birth and be counted.

So Joseph and Mary left their home in Nazareth to travel to the
town of Bethlehem. Joseph was of the family of King David and
Bethlehem was where they had lived. When they arrived, they
found the town was full of people who had come before them.
Mary's child would be born at any moment, but unhappily, Joseph
could find no room at any of the inns.

Finally, a kind-hearted innkeeper who didn't have a room for them in his inn, offered Joseph and Mary a stable where they could at least have shelter for the night.

There Mary gave birth to her son. She wrapped the little baby in
swaddling clothes and laid him in a manger where he could sleep.

Nearby, some shepherds were keeping watch over their sheep in
the fields. As they looked up, they saw the angel of the Lord
coming down to them. The glory of the Lord shone around them,
and the shepherds were very afraid.

And the angel said to the trembling shepherds: "Do not fear, for I have come to bring good news to you. This day a Savior has been born to you—the Messiah and Lord. You will find him in Bethlehem, a baby wrapped in swaddling clothes and lying in a manger."

Suddenly, there came the sounds of heavenly voices all around, praising God and saying, "Glory to God in heaven, and peace on earth."

When the angel had gone, the shepherds said to one another: "Let us go to Bethlehem and see this baby the Lord has told us about." They hurried to Bethlehem and found the stable where Mary and Joseph were with the baby.

After they saw the child, they understood, and the shepherds told everyone they saw about the baby and the angel. Returning to their flocks, the shepherds gave thanks and praise to God for all they had seen and heard.

"Glory to God in heaven,
and peace on earth."

Songs & Carols

Silent Night

Si - lent night, Ho - ly night,
Si - lent night, Ho - ly night,
Si - lent night, Ho - ly night,

All is calm, all is bright.
Shep - herds quake at the sight.
Son of God, love's pure light.

'Round yon Vir - gin Moth - er and Child
Glo - ries stream from heav - en a - far,
Ra - diant beams from Thy ho - ly face,

Ho - ly In - fant so ten - der and mild,
Heav'n - ly hosts sing Al - le - lu - ia;
With the dawn of re - deem - ing grace,

Sleep in heav - en - ly peace,_____
Christ the Sav - ior is born,_____
Je - sus, Lord, at Thy birth,_____

Sleep in heav - en - ly peace.
Christ the Sav - ior is born.
Je - sus, Lord, at Thy birth.

SILENT NIGHT

I Saw Three Ships

I SAW THREE SHIPS

Deck the Halls

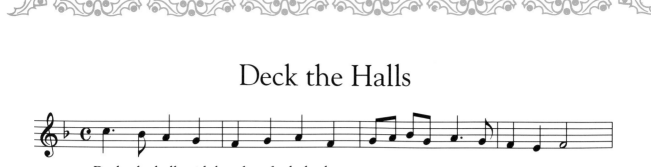

Deck the halls with boughs of hol - ly,

See the blaz - ing yule be - fore us, Fa - la-la-la - la, la - la - la - la.

Fast a - way the old year pass - es,

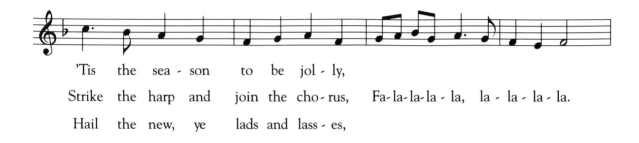

'Tis the sea - son to be jol - ly,

Strike the harp and join the cho - rus, Fa - la-la-la - la, la - la - la-la.

Hail the new, ye lads and lass - es,

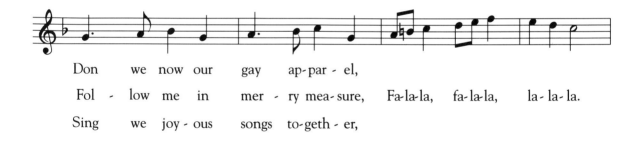

Don we now our gay ap-par - el,

Fol - low me in mer - ry mea - sure, Fa-la-la, fa-la-la, la-la-la.

Sing we joy - ous songs to-geth - er,

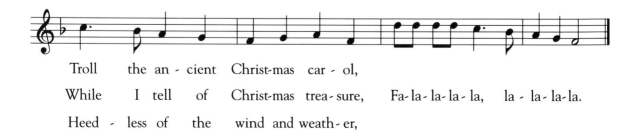

Troll the an - cient Christ-mas car - ol,

While I tell of Christ-mas trea - sure, Fa-la-la-la - la, la - la-la-la.

Heed - less of the wind and weath - er,

DECK THE HALLS

Jingle Bells

Dash-ing thru the snow in a one horse o-pen sleigh, O'er the hills we go
Day or two a - go I thought I'd take a ride, Soon Miss Fan nie Bright was

laugh-ing all the way; Bells on bob-tail ring, mak-ing spir - its bright, What
seat-ed by my side; The horse was lean and lank, mis -for-tune seemed our lot, He

fun it is to ride and sing a sleigh-ing song to - night.___Jin-gle bells,
got in-to a drift-ing bank and then we got up - sot.___

jin-gle bells, jin-gle all the way, Oh, what fun it is to ride in a one horse o-pen

sleigh; Jin-gle bells, jin-gle bells, jin-gle all the way, Oh, what fun it

1.
is to ride in a one horse o-pen sleigh.___ 2. one horse o-pen sleigh.

JINGLE BELLS

It Came Upon The Midnight Clear

It came up - on the mid - night clear, That glo - rious song— of
Still through the clo - ven skies they come, With peace - ful wings— un -
For lo! the days are hast - 'ning on, By proph - ets seen— of

old,— From an - gels bend - ing near the earth, To
furled;— And still their heav'n - ly mu - sic floats O'er
old,— When with the ev - er - cir - cling years, Shall

touch their harps— of gold:— "Peace on the earth,— good
all the wea - ry world;— A - bove its sad— and
come the time— fore - told,— When the new heaven— and

will to men, From heaven's— all gra - cious King."— The
lone - ly plains, They bend— on hov - er - ing wing,— And
earth shall own The Prince— of Peace their King,— And

world in sol - emn still - ness lay To hear the an - gels sing.—
ev - er o'er— its Ba - bel sounds The bless - ed an - gels sing.—
the whole world— send back the song Which now the an - gels sing.—

IT CAME UPON THE MIDNIGHT CLEAR

O Christmas Tree

O Christ - mas tree! O Christ - mas tree! How
O Christ - mas tree! O Christ - mas tree! You
O Christ - mas tree! O Christ - mas tree! Thy

faith - ful are thy branch - es.
are by all be - lov - ed.
can - dles shine so bright - ly!

Not on - ly green when sum - mer glows, But
How oft you've giv - en me de - light When
Their flick - 'ring flames send forth a light, Like

in the win - ter when it snows. O Christ - mas tree! O
Christ - mas fires were burn - ing bright! O Christ - mas tree! O
twink - ling stars that shine at night, O Christ - mas tree! O

Christ - mas tree! How faith - ful are thy branch - es.
Christ - mas tree! You are by all be - lov - ed.
Christ - mas tree! Thy can - dles shine so bright - ly!

O CHRISTMAS TREE

We Three Kings

We three kings of O - ri - ent are; Bear - ing gifts we
Born a King on Beth - le - hem plain, Gold we bring to

trav - erse a - far, Field and foun - tain, moor and
crown Him a - gain, King for - ev - er, ceas - ing

moun - tain, Fol - low - ing yon - der star. O,————
nev - er O - ver us all to reign.

star of won - der, star of night, Star with roy - al

beau - ty bright; West - ward lead - ing, still pro -

ceed - ing, Guide us to Thy per - fect light.

WE THREE KINGS

We Wish You a Merry Christmas

WE WISH YOU
A MERRY CHRISTMAS

C.Lit. PZ 5 .T85 1990
Greg Hildebrandt, ill.
'Twas the Night Before Christmas
& Other Holiday Favorites